ANIMAL INVENTORS

ANIMAL INVENTORS

by Thane Maynard

Photographs by Ron Austing

A First Book
FRANKLIN WATTS
NEW YORK / LONDON / TORONTO / SYDNEY
1991

This little book, my very first,
is dedicated with love to Kathleen Stewart,
a long-legged blond gal with the
eyes of a hawk and an Irish heart.

Cover art by Bryce Lee

Photographs by Ron Austing,
Cincinnati Zoo

Library of Congress Cataloging-in-Publication Data
Maynard, Thane.
Animal inventors / by Thane Maynard.
p. cm.—(A First book)
Includes bibliographical references and index.
Summary: Describes a variety of animal adaptations that inspired
humans to invent such items as the contact lens, seat cushion,
sonar, and the satellite dish.
ISBN 0-531-20051-5
1. Animals—Miscellanea—Juvenile literature. 2. Adaptation
(Biology)—Miscellanea—Juvenile literature. [1. Animals—
Miscellanea. 2. Adaptation (Biology)—Miscellanea.] I. Title.
II. Series.
QL49.M48 1991
591.5—dc20 91-14749 CIP AC

CONTENTS

ANIMAL INVENTORS

INTRODUCTION

For many millions of years, living things have been adapting, changing, and evolving for survival here on earth. Through this system of trial and error, wild plants and animals have developed ways to face the same conditions and dilemmas humans face. In many cases, their "inventions," or *adaptations,* are ones that we ourselves have borrowed to make our own survival easier.

Without observing birds in flight, we might never have had airplanes. Without geese, we would never have had down quilts and jackets to keep us warm. Without bats and whales, we might never have discovered sonar. And without insects like termites who feed on dead, rotting wood, we might never have caught on to the idea of recycling.

Scientists are still studying plants and animals today to learn from nature's tricks of the trade. There is far more we still don't yet know than there is that we do know for certain. Human beings have only been around for a few million years, so we still have a lot to learn about the world we share and how it works.

Animal Inventors takes a fun-loving look at the wonder of the natural world. It is a celebration of the life all around us, and the amazing ways animals cope with the conditions that surround them. Don't stop with just these few examples, though. There are thousands of such stories. Keep looking and you'll find other "inventors" and inventive ways wild creatures fit into their world—and ours.

And remember, the best way to learn about nature is to experience it. So, turn off your TV and *get outside*. The next thing you know, you might discover a new "invention" in your own backyard.

WHO INVENTED THE

SEAT CUSHION?

Here are some clues to the identity of the animal that first used a seat cushion:

- It spends most of its time sitting around.
- It is one of the most well-loved creatures in the world.
- It is a *marsupial*.
- It is one of the most lethargic animals known to exist.
- It comes from Australia.

By now, you must have guessed it is the koala. Koalas have a cushioning pad of fur on their bottom that is an inch thick and made of incredibly dense hair. The reason they need their own seat cushion is

Many monkeys, such as this Japanese macaque, have thick, hard skin on their rear end, making it easier for them to sit for long periods of time.

Left: Koalas spend nearly all of their time sitting in trees. Fortunately, they have a thick seat cushion made of very dense fur.

that koalas spend nearly their entire lives sitting still in trees. There is a great deal of debate about why koalas are so lazy. Some scientists believe it is principally due to the fact that there are no big *predators* for them to be wary of. Others feel that koalas sit around all the time because of where they live and what they eat. They live in eucalyptus trees and all they ever eat is eucalyptus leaves. This means they don't need to move all around the forest, as most animals do, searching for food. There is even some thought that the eucalyptus leaves themselves contain a low dosage of a tranquilizer, resulting in the slow *metabolism* of the koala. No matter the reason, koalas have a comfortable seat to rest on up in the gum trees of eastern Australia.

Koalas aren't the only creatures in need of a seat cushion, however. There are several kinds of *primates* that also spend the majority of their lives sitting down, and so have developed an extra thick skin patch, or callus, on their hindquarters. This is best demonstrated among the savannah-dwelling baboon *species,* such as the mandrill of West Africa and the olive baboon of East Africa. Scientists refer to these special pads as *ischial callosites.* Studies show that they provide maximum weight dispersion over the given area, working just like a human-made seat cushion.

HOW BIRDS ARE

ABLE TO FLY

It wasn't Wilbur and Orville Wright who invented the airplane wing. It wasn't Leonardo da Vinci either. It was the birds of the world who showed them all how to do it. An airplane wing works on precisely the same principle as the bird wing. Birds and planes both suffer from the dual constraints of *gravity* pulling them down and *drag* holding them back. They both need *lift* and *thrust*.

Everybody knows that planes have more thrust than birds, but in the lift department, the two are just alike. Both have wings that are rounded on the top and relatively flat, or sometimes concave on the bottom. This forces the air to move faster along the top, creating less air pressure above and resulting in lift.

If you don't think this is true, try this simple experiment. Hold a piece of paper right below your mouth so it hangs down over your fingers or thumbs. Now blow *downward* on the paper. Instead of the

Most bird wings, such as those of this pelican,
are built for flying. The wings are rounded
on the top of the leading edge, providing
lift as the bird glides through the air.

You can see that this Ruppell's
Vulture from Africa has wings shaped
just like an airplane's wings, even
when its "landing gear" is down.

paper flopping downward, as might be expected, it lifts upward. It rises up and, if you blow hard enough, actually flies through the air just the way a bird would.

The reason it works this way is called the *Bernoulli Principle,* named after the eighteenth-century Swiss mathematician Daniel Bernoulli. He was the first to discover that the higher the speed of a flowing gas or fluid, the lower the pressure. As the speed decreases, the pressure increases. (That's why you need to open up all the windows in your house if there's a tornado. With all the windows closed, your house could actually explode, as the pressure becomes so much greater inside than out.)

Using this same principle, a bird's wing gets natural lift, since the air pressure is considerably less on the top than on the bottom. This might make you think that nature has outsmarted us, but remember that modern birds have been flying for 100 million years. Their earliest ancestor, *Archeopteryx,* lived another fifty million years earlier. That's quite a head start, so just imagine how well our planes and spaceships will be able to fly by the time we catch up!

WHAT ANIMAL HAS

TASTE BUDS IN ITS FEET?

Most butterflies spend their lives drinking from flowers, using a very long tongue that they carry around coiled up at the base of their head. It would be difficult for them to unfurl this tongue and stick it down the throat of every flower they landed on just to taste if there was any nectar inside. Instead, when a butterfly lights on a flower, it can tell immediately how sweet that flower is by tasting it with its *feet*. Butterflies actually have taste buds in their feet. These "taste buds" are in the form of microscopic hairs that are, in fact, chemical receptors.

You've probably seen this in your own backyard. When a butterfly flits from flower to flower, landing for only a second at a time on some and then eventually choosing one to drink from, what it is actually doing is searching for the tastiest blossom. Now you know why they act that way. The petals of a flower taste good because of the nectar content, and the more

The "taste buds" of this coral hairstreak
butterfly are actually tiny, microscopic hairs
on the bottom of its feet. This allows it to
instantly taste the flowers it feeds on.

A tiger swallowtail butterfly drinking from
a thistle bloom. By tasting with its feet,
a butterfly can tell if there is much
nectar in a flower.

nectar, the more interested the butterfly will be in drinking from that particular flower instead of another.

All this flying around from blossom to blossom is powered in an unusual way since insects don't have any muscles in their wings. That's very different from vertebrates that fly, such as bats and birds, who have large masses of flight muscles in their chests as well as some muscles in their wings. Butterflies and other insects have rigid wings that are moved up and down by the muscles in their thorax. In fact, the wings actually pivot up and down on tiny fulcrums, or hinges, as the thorax muscles expand and contract.

WHO INVENTED THE DRINKING STRAW?

Did you ever wonder how an anteater or an aardvark can eat enough bugs to keep going? From lizards to lions, one of the most essential appendages of nearly any animal is its tongue.

The biggest tongue in the world belongs to the biggest animal in the world, the blue whale. Its tongue alone weighs more than an African elephant: twelve thousand pounds! Blue whales use their huge tongues to squish the water out of their mouths, trapping the remaining food with their baleen, the thin platelike filters that hang from their upper jaws. Sometimes called "whalebone," baleen is not bone at all, but is made of the same material as our fingernails. The favorite food of baleen whales is krill, tiny crustaceans resembling small shrimp that live by the billions in the oceans.

Believe it or not, it is the tiny animals, butterflies and moths, that have the largest tongues in proportion to their body size. Butterflies fluttering around your backyard have tongues over 2 inches (5 cm) long, the length of their entire bodies. That's the equivalent of a human with a tongue 6 feet (1.8 m) long!

Some butterflies and moths have tongues that are particularly amazing. In Madagascar, an island off the east coast of Africa, there lives a species of hawk-moth that drinks from deep-throated lilies and orchids. This 2-inch (5-cm) moth has a 9-inch (23 cm) tongue. In order to carry its tongue around, the moth coils it up, much like those birthday party favors that uncurl when we blow into one end of them. Butterflies and moths don't actually lap up their food, but use their tongues like a siphon, or drinking straw, to suck up the food so they can swallow it. What these insects are after is the sweet nectar from flowers, but they don't use tongue muscles to get it. The way it works is with the use of a special *hydraulic* system that allows the insects to maneuver their tongues about. As the tongue fills with fluid, it unfurls and becomes stiff enough for the insect to use just like a drinking straw. Then the tongue coils up again, and the insect takes off for other flowered meadows.

It is also through the use of extraordinary tongues that animals like anteaters and aardvarks are able to feed themselves. The giant anteater of South America has a tongue that sticks out twenty-four inches (.6 m) to lap up the ants it eats. Anteaters live on the forest

Hackberry butterflies will sometimes land
on people, apparently to sample our perspiration.
The tongue of many butterflies is as long
as its entire body.

When not in use, the "tongues" of butterflies and moths are curled up like a New Year's Eve party favor. This is a South American heliconius butterfly.

floor and are the only mammals with no teeth at all. Aardvarks, on the other hand, have flat, tubular teeth (located only in the back of their mouths) that they use to crunch up termites. But they catch those termites with the use of their oversized tongue.

Fortunately for people, aardvarks and anteaters can't bite us, but watch your step if they stick out their tongues!

WHO INVENTED

SONAR?

Ships use a sonar system to accurately determine the depth of the water or the location of schools of fish, but none of these human-made systems are as accurate as some of the amazing "sonar" techniques used in the natural world. Bats are famous for using *echolocation* to track down moths for dinner, but they certainly are not the only animals to use nature's sonar. Lots of sea creatures, from porpoises to beluga whales, use a similar system to find their prey. And there are even some birds who are thought to do the same thing.

Just as in human-made sonar systems, "echolocation" means that some animals are able to use sound waves to locate their prey. As with bats, the most common type of echolocation involves high-pitched sound waves. Basically, it works like this: When a bat is out on the hunt, it sends out sharp squeaks and uses its big ears to listen carefully for the echo these sounds create. By constantly sending out these squeaks, the bat can easily trace the movement and relative size of a flying insect. By listening

Big brown bats use their big ears to help
find their prey. Through echolocation, the
bats are able to track the flight of moths
and other insects, even in the dark.

to the echoes, the bat's sonar provides a "sound-picture" of its surroundings, enabling it to find its way, even in the pitch dark. Some bats can emit over 300 squeaks per second during the final part of the chase. The way they broadcast these sounds is just as amazing. Some bats, such as the leaf-nosed bat of Africa or the spear-nosed bat of South America, have huge noses, and they actually use them like megaphones to project their squeaks through the night. Many bats have a special ear covering that they are able to close when they are squeaking, so as not to hurt their ears. They also have to listen carefully, however, in order to locate that moth, so they are opening and closing their ears hundreds of times per minute.

The natural sonar of the bats is used for more than catching insects; it also tells the bats where they are in relation to other objects. For instance, one disconcerting thing to many people when they have a bat flying around their home is that even in the dark, the bat seems to be totally at ease, gracefully flying around and around, and never bumping into anything. Bats are so good at "seeing" in the dark with their sonar that researchers have filmed them flying through windows where parallel wires had been placed vertically at only 2-inch (5-cm) intervals. Instead of hitting their wings, the bats flew easily through the barriers every time by turning parallel to the wires at just the last second.

Bats can find their way, even in the dark,
with the help of their hearing. This little brown
bat listens to the echoes bounced off objects
in its surroundings in order to keep from
hitting anything while in flight.

The moths of the world are doing their best to "jam" the sonar of approaching bats. The fuzzier the moth, the less bounce it gives to the squeak of the bat. It is just like bouncing a ball on a hard surface—such as a sidewalk—as compared to a soft surface, such as your bed.

The echolocation of porpoises and whales is used in a similar way. However, these creatures project the sounds out of their forehead from an area called the "melon," and actually receive sounds through their chin. The sound vibrations are then transmitted along the jaw up to the inner ear.

Since sound waves travel so well in water, they can be incredibly accurate. Some porpoises, in fact, have been known to actually identify different species of fish, just by using sonar!

The inner ears of dolphins and whales are on the sides of their heads, just like ours, but since they have no external ears, you might think sounds would pass right by them. However, they have the special ability to pick up sound vibrations in the water on the leading edge of their bodies, with their jaws. The sound travels inside the jaw bone up to the ear drum through a thin oil.

With an estimated 30,000 different fishes in the world, that is no small accomplishment. (Of course, porpoises cannot identify 30,000 different fishes!)

WHO INVENTED UNDERWEAR?

Never underestimate the role that underwear plays in the natural scheme of things. For instance, it is the reason why naturalists everywhere are sincere when they tell concerned nature lovers not to worry when they see songbirds nesting in the yard in the middle of winter. Even on a cold or rainy day, the birds' feathers will—and do—keep them warm.

Nature has a way of preparing all its creatures for the weather wherever they live. In the case of *warm-blooded* animals such as mammals and birds, that means protective underwear. In some mammals, it is usually in the form of thick, soft fur underneath the outer guard hairs. In birds, it is the soft down feathers right next to their skin. These work just like the insulation in your house, trapping a layer of air in the walls, holding the warmth in and the cold out. It is also why down jackets and fur coats are so warm.

But did you know that some animals wear their

Even on the coldest days of winter,
this pair of mourning doves is able to
stay warm because of the insulation
provided by their down feathers.

underwear on the inside of their skin? That's why some animals, such as most of the *aquatic* mammals from hippos to walruses and even whales, seem so tubby. They use the fat layers underneath their skin to insulate them against the cold of the water. It works like a built-in wet suit to help the animal keep warm. For instance, people have a total body-fat content of about 12 percent, while whales have as much as 25 percent body fat. On a 150,000-pound (68,000-kg) blue whale, that's 37,500 pounds (17,000 kg) of fat!

But birds, people, and other warm-blooded mammals are in the minority. The vast majority of the earth's creatures are *cold-blooded* and don't keep much warmth in, since they don't generate much heat. Instead, their body temperature is controlled by their surroundings. This is why snakes, turtles, and other cold-blooded creatures often lie in the sun, soaking up heat from warm rocks, when they would other-wise be hiding. In the wintertime, it is just the oppo-site. In order to stay warm, they have to hide from the cold air.

As for us, the next time you slip into your "long johns," remember that we didn't invent underwear—we just borrowed a trick from the animal world. In fact, when you think about it, people are one of the few animals that are not only born naked, but re-

Bird "underwear." Beneath the outer
contour feathers on the belly of this barred
owl lie the bird's down feathers.

main naked throughout their entire lives, with no natural body covering, or underwear. From the smallest bird to the greatest whale, all other animals have something in common—a way to beat the extreme temperatures in nature.

WHO INVENTED CONTACT LENSES?

The idea of contact lenses, curiously enough, originated with the snakes of the world, who would seem to be at a great disadvantage since they cannot shut their eyes. In fact, snakes have no eyelids at all. But they do have contact-lens-like scales that grow over their eyeballs, allowing their eyes to stay moist while at the same time protecting them from damage. It should be noted that this eye-protective scale has been developed for a different reason than human contact lenses. Ours serve the same purpose as eyeglasses, to correct our vision.

If you find a snake skin in the woods, if you look closely you'll see that the snake sheds its contact lenses as well. Each time a snake sheds, it grows a new protective scale to cover its eyes. This is also how you can tell if a snake is about to turn in its old skin for new. The newer the scales, the clearer they are. But as a snake approaches the time to cast off its old

Snakes do not have eyelids. They cannot
blink or wink, but they protect their eyes and
keep them moist with a clear scale that is
replaced when the snake sheds its skin.

This rhinoceros viper from Africa has
eyes that are well-hidden, helping it
to blend in better with its surroundings
as it sneaks up on its prey.

skin, the scales all over its body begin to dry out and become milky-looking and translucent. A snake that is ready to shed has very cloudy eyes.

Snakes are not the only creatures with protective eye wear. Birds, crocodiles, alligators, and even some frogs have a third eyelid which they use for rapid blinking and to keep things out of their eyes. This is called the nictitating membrane and serves as a sort of zoological windshield wiper. Perhaps the alligators and other crocodilians are the most ingenious of all because they use theirs like swimming goggles. They actually hold their third eyelid closed while underwater. This allows them to see farther, just as when we wear a mask or goggles. It's more important for them, however, because they have to catch their dinner as they swim.

WHO INVENTED SNOWSHOES?

All my friends who live in Alaska wear snowshoes in the dead of winter. They stole this idea from a variety of arctic animals who spend their lives in the snow. For animals, just like people, the purpose of this special footwear is to keep from sinking up to their bellies in snow. Most famous may be the animal named for this phenomenon, the snowshoe hare, a very quick rabbit species with large hind feet that help it make a quick getaway even when others are snowbound. In fact, snowshoe hares literally run across the top of the snow! Their getaway is vital, because close behind may be a Canadian lynx in hot pursuit.

The blue ribbon in the snowshoe competition should probably go to the northern cat species. Big cats like the Siberian tiger and the elusive snow leopard certainly qualify as having well-adapted feet, but the grand prize may go to a small cat, the Northern lynx. There are different *subspecies* on different con-

As the name implies, snow leopards are built
for life in the snow. Even their feet, which
are large and partially covered with fur on
the bottom, are well-adapted to the snow.

The feet of the Siberian lynx help it make
its way, even through incredibly deep snow.

tinents. In North America, they're called Canadian lynx, and in Asia and Russia they're known as Siberian lynx, but both spend over half their lives in the snow and use the same method to get around as humans do when we don snowshoes. The lynx have big feet on which the toes spread out, with the hairs keeping the snow from passing between the toes while the animals search for food.

Other mammals have great winter hiking gear as well. For instance, the polar bear has the largest feet of all eight bear species; they are even equipped with a hairy, "nonskid" bottom so they won't slip on the ice. Smaller animals, such as the ermine, opt to travel under the surface of the snow, sometimes popping up through the snow like dolphins in the water.

WHO INVENTED THE

CRASH HELMET?

Just imagine the life of a woodpecker. They bang their heads into trees all day long, often thousands of times per day, and never get a headache! They aren't just tapping the tree either; they are hitting it as hard as they can, just as hard as you would be able to hit the palm of one hand with the fist of the other. How they are able to do this is unique in the animal kingdom; they each have their own crash helmet.

Woodpeckers have a very thickwalled skull in order to withstand the constant shock of chiseling away at trees. To help absorb impact, they each have a pad of cartilagelike tissue at the base of their bill. This cushioning pad is about the thickness of a dime and runs from the bird's bill down to its neck in order to properly distribute the shock. This pad works on the same principle as our own motorcycle, football, or hockey helmets, except that our artificial padding is usually either fluid-filled or foam rubber of some kind.

To build nests and find insects, this red-bellied woodpecker taps hard and often on trees. It is able to withstand the impact thanks to the way its head is built.

Woodpeckers also come equipped with very strong muscles in their necks, stretching up to the bills, which aid in absorbing the constant pounding.

Woodpeckers as well have specialized feet. Like most birds, they have four toes on each foot. But with most birds, the three front toes face forward, the fourth toward the back. This enables birds to perch more easily on top of branches. The woodpecker's foot, on the other hand, has two toes facing forward and two facing back. This allows them to easily support themselves on the side of the tree while they peck away at the wood.

The tail of a woodpecker also plays a role in its life-style. The extremely stiff tail feathers are used to prop the bird up against a tree. This anchoring keeps the woodpecker from knocking itself loose while pecking.

Woodpeckers are after two things when they are chiseling away at trees. One is food and the other is a nesting site. The food comes in the form of insects—both adults and larvae—that hide inside the trunk of a tree or just under the bark.

Woodpecker's nests are hard-won indeed. The birds excavate a tree cavity to make a place to incubate their eggs and care for their young. It certainly takes more work to build this kind of nest than some of the simpler systems used by other birds.

WHO INVENTED THE SATELLITE DISH?

What animal would you say has the best hearing in the world? You probably assume it's one with big ears, like an elephant, or bat, or desert jack rabbit? But believe it or not, the best hearing in the world belongs to an animal whose ears you can't even see: the barn owl! Owls have such highly tuned hearing that they can locate their prey in the dark, not an easy job since the animals they eat are, literally, quiet as mice!

Barn owls have the best hearing of all animals because of their anatomy. You may not be able to see its ears, but the owl is able to hear so well because its entire face works like an ear, picking up sounds. Underneath all those feathers on its face lies a skull that is concave. You could say that the barn owl invented the satellite dish because its hearing works in the same way. Sound is scooped up by its dish-shaped skull and then directed to its ears from

Thanks to their hearing, barn owls can locate
and catch mice even in complete darkness.
The owls' faces are concave and can "scoop
up" even the slightest sound.

A long-eared owl taking off in search
of dinner. All owls have acute hearing,
which enables them to listen for
the movement of their prey.

the ridge of feathers and the beak in the middle of its face. One of their ears faces slightly forward and upward while the other is tilted downward and to the rear. All of this makes for a unique kind of hearing ability that allows a barn owl to hunt in complete darkness. Weighing less than one pound each, barn owls eat only small rodents like the white-footed mouse and the meadow vole, which are especially hard to spot in a prairie or abandoned field in the middle of the night.

Unfortunately, barn owls are endangered throughout much of their original geographical range in North America. Their only source of food is small rodents that live in old fields and meadows. But as those areas become more intensively plowed and developed, the mice flee, and there is nothing left for the barn owl to hunt. Fortunately, barn owls breed well in captivity. It is hoped that through the combined efforts of setting up preserves and releasing captive-bred birds there, barn owls will continue to survive in their native habitat where they can fly free.

WHO INVENTED THE SAFETY ROPE?

Rock climbers, tree surgeons, and window washers all use safety ropes, just in case they fall. They borrowed a page from the handbook of some of the tree-dwelling animals of the world, the ones with prehensile tails. The term "prehensile" comes from the Latin word, *prehensus,* meaning "grasped." That's exactly how zoologists use the word, as well. A prehensile tail or tongue is one that can wrap around an object and hold on.

In the tail department, monkeys get most of the publicity. Actually, only some of the monkeys from Central and South America have prehensile tails. Old World monkeys from Africa and Asia cannot grasp with their tails at all. But the monkeys that do have prehensile tails can do a great variety of tricks. When running and leaping through the trees, they will actually use their tail as if it were a fifth hand, sometimes even letting go with their feet and temporarily holding on with their tails alone.

The kinkajou from Central and South America
is a cousin of the raccoon. Its grasping tail
serves as an extra "hand" when it climbs trees.

Left: The Virginia oppossum has
a prehensile tail.

Other famous tail owners include the opposum from the United States and the bear cat, or binturong, from Southeast Asia (which, by the way, is the only Old World mammal with a grasping tail). Another interesting animal is the kinkajou, a cousin of the raccoon, that lives in Central and South America. It is the animal that, in a way, first invented the safety rope, because it uses its tail while hanging upside down in order to get to its favorite treat—the termite. Unlike termites that live in North America, many tropical varieties are *arboreal,* or tree-dwelling. Since kinkajous *also* live in trees, the only way they can free up their front feet to scratch open a termite nest for a meal is to hang by their tail and hind feet.

You could say the point of this story is that a tail is a great thing to hang on to—particularly when you're up a tree!

GLOSSARY

Adaptation—the special traits a plant or animal has for survival in its native home.

Arboreal—tree-dwelling.

Aquatic—an animal or plant adapted to living in water.

Bernoulli principle—the principle in physics that states that the faster a gas or fluid flows past an object, the lighter the pressure; this is why airplane and bird wings are shaped the way they are.

Cold-blooded—having a body temperature that is determined by the surroundings or environment.

Drag—the force of resistance that slows or hinders the forward progress of birds in flight.

Echolocation—the system used by insect-eating bats to locate their prey; they send out a series of rapid clicks that echo, or bounce, off objects in their path, telling the bats the location of their prey.

Gravity—the natural force that causes weight, pulling objects down toward the earth.

Hydraulic—operated by the pressure transmitted when a liquid is forced through a tube; butterflies and moths manipulate their tongues in this manner.

Marsupial—kangaroos and related animals with pouches for carrying their young.

Metabolism—the processes by which substances are handled in a living body.

Predator—an animal, such as a cat, snake, or hawk, that eats other animals.

Primate—the order of mammals that includes monkeys, apes, prosimians, and humans.

Species—one type or kind of plant or animal, potentially able to breed with one another.

Subspecies—separate groups within a species of plant or animal, adapted to different environments (examples: Bengal tigers, Siberian tigers, and Indo-Chinese tigers).

Warm-blooded—able to maintain relatively high and constant body temperature.

FOR FURTHER
READING

Caras, Roger. *Animal Architecture.* Richmond, Virginia: Westover Publishing Company, 1971.

Harvey, Edmund, Ed. *Reader's Digest Book of Facts.* Montreal: Reader's Digest Association, 1987.

McGrath, Susan. *The Amazing Things Animals Do.* Washington, D.C.: National Geographic, 1989.

Pope, Joyce. *Do Animals Dream? Children's Questions About Animals Most Often Asked of The British Natural History Museum.* London: Viking Kestrel, 1986.

Robinson, David. *Living Wild: The Secrets of Animal Survival.* Washington, D.C.: National Wildlife Federation, 1980.

Wood, Gerald. *Animal Facts & Feats: A Guinness Book of World Records.* New York: Sterling Publishing Company, 1977.

World Wildlife Fund. *The Atlas of World Wildlife.* London: Portland House, 1973.

Periodicals

Zoobooks, Box 85271, San Diego, California 92138.

Ranger Rick, National Wildlife Federation, Washington, D.C.

World Magazine, National Geographic Society, Washington, D.C.

INDEX

61

ABOUT THE

Thane Maynard grew up in the low country swamps of central Florida, in the days before condominiums, VCRs, shopping malls, and Disney World. As a result, he spent his youth catching scarlet king snakes and baby alligators, while developing his love of nature and wildlife.

Mr. Maynard is director of conservation at the Cincinnati Zoo & Botanical Garden, where he has worked since 1977. He is also host of the daily radio feature "The 90-Second Naturalist" on National Public Radio and the television series "Animals in Action" and "Secrets at the Zoo."